DRAGON MASTERS

BLOOM OF THE FLOWER DRAGON

BY

TRACEY WEST

SCHOLASTIC INC.

DRAGON MASTERS

Read All the Adventures

1
2
3
4
5
6
7
8
9
10
11
12
13
14
15
16
17
18
19
20
21
22

Special Edition!

More books coming soon!

TABLE OF CONTENTS

FOR ALL OF MY ENTHUSIASTIC READERS

in Germany, a land rich in dragon lore. — TW

Text copyright © 2022 by Tracey West
Illustrations copyright © 2022 by Scholastic Inc.

Library of Congress Cataloging-in-Publication Data

Names: West, Tracey, 1965- author. Howells, Graham, illustrator.
Title: Bloom of the flower dragon / by Tracey West ; illustrated by Graham Howells.
Description: First edition. | New York, NY : Branches/Scholastic Inc., 2022.|
Series: Dragon masters ; [21]| Audience: Ages 6-8. Audience:
Grades 2-3. | Summary: Drake and the other Dragon Masters help Wildroot, a Flower Dragon whose home is in danger, find his Dragon Master Oskar after Oskar's identity is revealed to them by the Dragon Stone.
Identifiers: LCCN 2021031820 (print)| ISBN 9781338776874 (paperback)| ISBN 9781338776881 (library binding)
Subjects: CYAC: Dragons—Fiction. | Magic—Fiction. | Wizards—Fiction. Adventure and adventurers—Fiction. | BISAC: JUVENILE FICTION / Readers/ Chapter Books JUVENILE FICTION / Action & Adventure / General | LCGFT: Novels.
Classification: LCC PZ7.W51937 Bj 2022 (print) DDC [Fic]—dc23
LC record available at https://lccn.loc.gov/2021031820

10 9 8 7 6 5 4 3 2 1   22 23 24 25 26

Printed in China   62

First edition, April 2022
Illustrated by Graham Howells
Edited by Katie Carella
Book design by Sarah Dvojack

THE DRAGON VISITOR

orm, we have a visitor!" Drake said.

Worm — a big, brown Earth Dragon — opened his eyes. He had been napping next to Drake.

Drake showed Worm the tiny dragon perched on his hand. White flower petals sprouted on the head, wings, and tail of the little green dragon.

"Have you ever seen a dragon this size?" Drake asked. The green chunk of Dragon Stone around his neck glowed, like it always did when he communicated with his dragon.

He heard Worm's reply inside his head. *It looks like a type of Flower Dragon.*

Just then, a shadow crossed over them. Drake looked up to see three dragons flying above the Valley of Clouds.

First came Bo, riding on the winds with his blue Water Dragon, Shu.

Next came Ana, flying gracefully with Kepri, her white Sun Dragon.

Finally, Rori and her red Fire Dragon, Vulcan, zoomed down from the sky.

The three dragons landed in the grass. Their Dragon Masters climbed down and ran toward Drake and Worm.

"Drake, you're back!" Bo cried.

"Did you stop Astrid?" asked Ana.

Rori spotted the Flower Dragon. "Did you bring that dragon back with you?"

Drake took a deep breath. "There's a lot to tell you," he said. The last two days had been very busy. Drake, several Dragon Masters, and dozens of wizards had tried to stop a wizard named Astrid from casting a terrible spell. She wanted to bring the bones of ancient beasts to life and take over the world.

"Astrid cast the spell," Drake began. "She brought the bones to life at the Fortress of the Stone Dragon. Then she took her army to King Albin's kingdom."

Ana gasped. "How did you stop her?"

Drake explained how Dragon Masters Mina and her Ice Dragon, Frost, and Caspar and his Stone Dragon, Shaka, had helped Drake and Worm defeat Astrid.

"In the end, Shaka turned Astrid into stone," Drake finished.

Bo, Ana, and Rori listened to the story with wide eyes.

"I'm glad you stopped Astrid," Rori said.

"Me, too," Bo agreed. "But where's Griffith? Didn't he come back with you?"

Griffith the wizard taught Drake, Ana, Bo, and Rori how to work with their dragons. They all lived in King Roland's castle, just behind the Valley of Clouds.

GRIFFITH

"Griffith is helping to bring Astrid to the Wizard's Council prison," Drake replied. "Even though she's a statue now, this will make sure she'll never hurt anyone again."

Ana moved closer to the Flower Dragon. "You still haven't told us where you found this little cutie."

"This dragon found *me*," Drake replied. "Worm and I had just gotten back when this Flower Dragon climbed onto my arm. But I don't know where he came from."

Suddenly, Drake's Dragon Stone began to glow. Then he heard Worm's voice in his mind.

The Flower Dragon is reaching out to me, Worm said. *His name is Wildroot. He says he needs our help!*

CHAPTER 2

WILDROOT'S TALE

Wildroot continued to communicate with Worm. Drake listened to Worm's voice in his head:

Wildroot lives near the village of Stellburg, in the Lofty Mountains. He says his tribe is in danger.

Then Drake told his friends what he'd heard.

"A tribe? Does he live with a whole group of Flower Dragons?" Bo asked.

Suddenly, a picture popped into Drake's mind, and he knew Worm was sending it. Drake saw a green field studded with star-shaped white flowers. Tiny green dragons slept and played among the flowers.

Wildroot's tribe lives in this field of rare starflowers.

Then a picture appeared of a creature no taller than the flowers. She wore a gown made of golden-brown leaves, the same color as her wrinkled skin. She had leafy wings, too.

Is that a fairy? Drake asked Worm.

Brighteye is a forest sprite and a friend to the Flower Dragons. She can see into the future. And in a vision, she saw a terrible monster heading for Stellburg.

A new picture appeared in Drake's head: two red, glowing eyes peering out of a dark forest. He gasped.

Brighteye told the tribe they would need help to defeat the monster. She told them of the brave dragons of Bracken Castle and their Dragon Masters, who help others. Wildroot volunteered and came here.

The picture vanished. Drake told his friends what he had seen and heard.

"Wildroot came to the right place!" Rori cried. "We'll help him!"

Wildroot says the red-eyed monster will reach Stellburg in a day or two, Worm told Drake. *There is not much time.*

"We should go inside," Bo suggested. "Griffith has maps in his workshop that can help us."

"And Rori and I will look for books about Flower Dragons in the classroom," Ana added.

They traveled through the tunnel connecting the Valley of Clouds to Bracken Castle.

Worm, Shu, Kepri, and Vulcan went into the Dragon Caves to rest. Wildroot perched on Drake's shoulder.

Then Drake and Bo entered Griffith's workshop. Books and magical items filled the shelves. On a table was a wooden box carved with dragons. It held a large piece of the Dragon Stone. This magical stone chose those who were ready to become Dragon Masters.

Bo picked up a book and leafed through the pages. "I'll see if I can find the Lofty Mountains," he muttered as he searched. Then he stopped and smiled. "Got it! Here they are, and here is Stellburg!"

Drake looked at the map. Stellburg sat all by itself on one of the mountains. The bottom of the map showed a castle and a large forest. "The Dark Forest," he read out loud. "That looks sort of spooky."

Bo pointed to an area on the map close to Stellburg. "There's the field of starflowers!"

THE LOFTY MOUNTAINS

HIGHTOP

STELLBURG

SCHNEALAND

GRAYSTONE CASTLE

GRINWALD

VALLEY OF STARFLOWERS

THE DARK FOREST

HIRSHBURG

FINSTER HOLLOW

"Perfect!" Drake cried. "I'll go get Worm, so we can —"

The lid of the carved box suddenly flew open. Then a burst of bright, green light shot from Griffith's Dragon Stone!

A NEW DRAGON MASTER?

Moving pictures appeared inside the Dragon Stone's light.

Drake and Bo watched a boy with blond, wavy hair stroll along a hilly path. He wore a brown vest over a pale purple tunic.

Just then, Rori and Ana ran into Griffith's workshop.

"We saw the light!" Rori cried.

15

"The Dragon Stone turned on all of a sudden," Bo replied. "Look!"

The blond boy passed a building with a sign over the door: THE STELLBURG INN.

"Stellburg!" Drake cried. "That's near where Wildroot is from. Do you think —"

"The Dragon Stone is showing us Wildroot's Dragon Master!" Rori cried, jumping up and down.

Wildroot scrambled over to the stone. He looked up at the image of the boy, his eyes wide.

Then the green light faded.

"I think this means we're supposed to find Wildroot's Dragon Master," Ana said.

"We need a plan," Bo said. "But first, I will go to the kitchen and bring us some food so we don't have to stop for dinner."

"Good idea, Bo," Drake replied. "I'll go get Worm. We need to know if Wildroot recognized that boy."

A few minutes later, the four Dragon Masters were seated around the table in their classroom. Wildroot sat on the tabletop, and Worm fit his large head through the door. Bo passed around a plate of bread, cheese, and apples.

"I wonder if Wildroot is hungry," Drake said. "Worm, what do Flower Dragons eat?"

Worm looked at Wildroot. Seconds later, Drake heard Worm's voice in his head.

Drake told the others, "Wildroot says he got plenty of sunshine today, so he's not hungry."

Ana smiled. "Flower Dragons eat sunshine? Wait until Wildroot sees what Kepri can do."

Drake smiled, too. Then he turned to Worm. "Can you please ask Wildroot if he has seen the boy in the Dragon Stone before?"

His Dragon Stone glowed.

Wildroot says no. The Flower Dragons stay hidden from humans.

Drake reported this to his friends.

"Maybe we need Wildroot's Dragon Master to help us fight the monster?" Rori guessed.

Bo nodded. "That sounds right."

Drake looked at Wildroot. "We will go to Stellburg first thing in the morning to find his Dragon Master!"

TO THE VILLAGE!

The next morning, Drake awoke with the little Flower Dragon curled up beside him. Wildroot yawned.

The tiny dragon scuttled over to the window. He lifted his face and closed his eyes as the sun hit his scales. He smiled.

Bo sat up in his bed and laughed. "Wildroot's eating breakfast," he said, and then his stomach rumbled. "I could use some breakfast, too!"

Drake and Bo got dressed for the day. Drake picked up Wildroot and they made their way to the Dragon Masters' dining room. Rori and Ana were already there, and so was Griffith!

"Good morning, Drake and Bo," Griffith said. "You'll be happy to know that Astrid is safely locked away in the Wizard's Council prison."

He stepped closer to Wildroot. "So this is the Flower Dragon Rori and Ana just told me about," he said. "You are a fine-looking dragon, Wildroot!"

Then the wizard clapped his hands. "Drake, I think Ana should go with you and Wildroot to Stellburg. Since Flower Dragons like sunshine, Kepri might be useful."

"Hooray!" Ana exclaimed.

"Rori and Bo, you'll stay with me. I've been away for some time and there is much to do here at the castle," Griffith said. "Now, everyone, let's eat! The cook made currant buns."

Drake sat down and picked up a bun dotted with purple berries. "Griffith, we're going to try to find the boy in the Dragon Stone as soon as we get to Stellburg," he said, taking a bite.

"That is smart," Griffith replied. "There is a reason my stone showed you the boy."

After breakfast, they all went to the Dragon Caves. Worm and Kepri came out of their caves.

"Worm, we need to transport to the village of Stellburg," Drake announced.

Then Drake heard Worm's voice in his head:

Wildroot is worried. He says the villagers do not know about Flower Dragons. His tribe lives a quiet life, hidden among the starflowers. And they like it that way.

Drake told the others about Wildroot's fear.

Griffith extended his right pointer finger and sparks shot out. A cloth pouch with a strap magically appeared.

"Wildroot can hide in this bag," Griffith said.

"Thanks!" Drake said. "Worm, let Wildroot know."

Wildroot climbed inside and Drake slung it over his shoulder. Griffith handed Drake a green Dragon Stone that dangled from a gold chain.

"Give this to the new Dragon Master when you meet him," Griffith instructed.

Drake nodded. "Yes, Griffith." He tucked the stone into his pocket.

Then he and Ana touched Worm, and Ana touched Kepri.

"Worm, take us to Stellburg!" Drake cried.

Worm transported them in a flash of light.

Drake blinked. They had landed in the middle of a village square. Behind them was a carved wooden statue of a winged dragon as big as Worm. Drake read the plaque at its base.

THE LEGENDARY DRAGON OF STELLBURG

"The Legendary Dragon of Stellburg," he said.

Suddenly, villagers surrounded them. They pointed at Worm and Kepri.

"Dragons!" a man yelled.

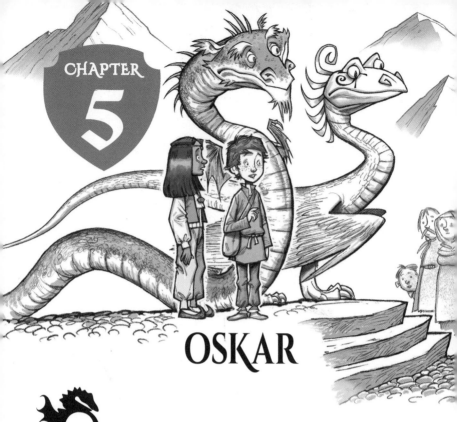

OSKAR

Our dragons are friendly!" Drake told the villagers who had gathered around them.

"Yes, please don't be scared," Ana added.

A woman stepped forward. "We are not afraid of your dragons," she said. "It is good to see dragons in our village again."

Drake pointed to the statue. "Did that winged dragon once live here?"

CHAPTER 5

THE LEGENDARY DRAGON
OF STELLBURG

She nodded. "Yes, she did. You see, all kinds of dangerous creatures live in the Lofty Mountains. That great dragon protected Stellburg from them. But we have not had a dragon protector here for a hundred years."

Ana looked at Drake, and he gazed down at his bag. They would have to explain things without giving up the secret of the Flower Dragons.

"We have come here because of a very special dragon," Drake announced.

"Yes, and we are looking for the boy who has been chosen to become this dragon's Dragon Master," Ana added.

"We don't know the boy's name, but he should be eight years old," Drake said.

"With blond, wavy hair," Ana added.

The woman turned to the villagers. "Boys, come forward!"

Six boys made their way to the front of the crowd. All of them had blond, wavy hair. But Drake and Ana recognized the boy from the Dragon Stone.

Drake pointed at him. "The Dragon Stone has chosen you to be a Dragon Master."

"My name is Oskar," he said, grinning with excitement. He looked up at Worm and Kepri. "Which of these fine dragons shall I be master of?"

Drake wasn't sure what to say. Then he heard Worm's voice:

Wildroot would like to meet Oskar. He is not afraid anymore.

"Your dragon is right here," Drake told Oskar, and he opened his bag. Wildroot crawled onto Drake's arm. "This is Wildroot."

Oskar frowned. "That is my dragon? Are you kidding me?"

A MYSTERY

The villagers all started to talk at once. Drake even heard some laughter.

"What kind of a dragon is that?"

"It's too small to be a dragon!"

Ana motioned to Oskar. "We should go somewhere quieter to talk about this."

"Follow me," Oskar replied. "But I can't talk long. I've got something very important to do."

Oskar led them outside the village square, past the Stellburg Inn and buildings where food, clothing, and other goods were for sale. Then Oskar stopped next to a field of grazing sheep.

"All right," he said. "Who are you, and what do you want?"

"I am Ana, and this is my dragon, Kepri," Ana answered. "And this is Drake and his dragon, Worm. We're from the Kingdom of Bracken."

"Wildroot here is a Flower Dragon from these mountains," Drake explained. "He traveled to find us because his tribe needs help. A monster is headed this way."

Oskar frowned. "A monster?"

"Yes," Ana replied. "And if we all work together, we can stop it."

"But we can't do it without you," Drake added. "You and Wildroot need to learn how to work together. As his Dragon Master, you can help him tap into his powers."

Oskar pointed to the backpack he wore. "Can't you handle this without me? I'm on my way to Graystone Castle, to find my father."

"Where did he go?" Ana asked.

"One month ago, he went on an errand to the castle, and he hasn't come back," Oskar replied. "I'm afraid something terrible has happened to him!"

THE VALLEY OF STARFLOWERS

Oskar began to walk away. "Sorry I can't help you!" he said.

"I have an idea!" Ana called out to him. "If you come with us to help the Flower Dragons, then we will help you find your father."

Oskar stopped. "Really?"

"Yes," Drake replied. "Worm can transport us to that castle in the blink of an eye. You won't have to walk there."

"Can we go to Graystone first?" Oskar asked.

Drake shook his head. "No, we must hurry to stop the monster."

Oskar looked thoughtful. Then he nodded. "Okay, let's get going! The sooner we learn what this monster is all about, the sooner we will find my father."

Drake took the Dragon Stone from his pocket and put it around Oskar's neck. "This will help you communicate with Wildroot. We will explain on the way."

Wildroot hopped onto Worm's neck.

Wildroot will show me the way, Worm told Drake. *We will take the lead.*

As they walked away from the village, Drake touched his Dragon Stone.

"Did you see how my Dragon Stone just glowed, Oskar?" Drake asked. "The stone allows Dragon Masters and their dragons to understand each other. I can hear Worm's voice in my head. He can hear my voice, too."

"Oskar, why don't you try communicating with Wildroot?" Ana suggested.

Oskar looked down at his Dragon Stone. "Okay," he said. "Hey, Wildroot! Why are you so small?"

Ana glanced at Drake and shook her head.

Oskar waited. "Not glowing! I think your magical stone picked the wrong boy for this little dragon."

Worm, does Wildroot feel any connection at all to Oskar? Drake asked.

He says that Oskar is a turnip-head, Worm replied.

Drake sighed. "I don't think these two will ever connect," he whispered to Ana.

They walked for about an hour down the side of the mountain. Worm stopped as a valley opened up before them.

"This is the Valley of Starflowers," Oskar remarked, gazing all around. "It's where the grandmothers come to collect flowers for tea."

Tiny white flowers dotted the green grass as far as they could see.

"How beautiful!" Ana whispered.

Wildroot stood on his back legs. He began to sing. *Ooh, ooh, ooh, ooh, ahhhhhhh*...

The air sparkled with glittery mist, and dozens of Flower Dragons appeared among the flowers.

Drake gasped. "I've never seen so many dragons before!"

LEGEND OF THE WEREWOLF

The Flower Dragons swarmed around the Dragon Masters and their dragons. They made excited chirping sounds. They seemed to be communicating with Wildroot.

"Worm, why didn't we see the Flower Dragons at first?" Drake asked.

Wildroot says that Flower Dragons release a special mist. The mist keeps humans from seeing them. When Wildroot sang, the dragons stopped the illusion.

"That is an amazing power!" Ana said.

Even Oskar seemed impressed. "Yes, that is a pretty good trick."

Drake heard Worm again:

The Flower Dragons get all their powers from drinking starflower nectar. These flowers and dragons are connected.

As Drake repeated this news, a tiny creature flew up to the newcomers.

Drake recognized her as the forest sprite that Wildroot had shown Worm.

"Are you Brighteye?" he asked. "The Flower Dragons' friend who can see the future?"

She bowed her head in greeting. "Indeed I am. I live with others of my kind in the nearby forest. We look out for the Flower Dragons."

Drake and Ana introduced themselves and their dragons.

Brighteye smiled. "You are the Dragon Masters of Bracken! The ones who help others."

"I am Oskar and I'm not from Bracken," Oskar said. "I am Wildroot's Dragon Master. Or at least, that's what Drake says."

Wildroot jumped off Worm, dashed over to Brighteye, and started to chirp.

"Wait, do you and the dragons understand one another?" Drake asked the forest sprite.

Brighteye's golden eyes twinkled. "When you are as old as I am, you understand many things."

"Wildroot told us you saw a vision of a red-eyed monster," Ana said. "And that you need our help."

The fairy nodded. "I fear that the Flower Dragons and the people of the village are in great danger. Let us see where the monster is now."

She produced a twig from her belt and moved it in circles. A ring of golden fairy dust formed in the air. Inside the glittering ring, an image of a spooky cave appeared. Red, glowing eyes peered from within. Then the creature let out an eerie howl.

Drake shivered.

"I know that howl," Brighteye said. "This monster is a werewolf. It will be here soon."

She waved her wand, and the fairy ring—and the image inside—disappeared.

"I know what a wolf is, but what's a werewolf?" Drake asked.

Oskar spoke up. "Everyone in Stellburg knows about werewolves," he said. "They are fierce, hungry monsters much larger than wolves. A werewolf eats anything that moves."

"Yes," Brighteye said. "But the werewolf is also a poor, cursed creature. White berries called moonberries grow in the deepest part of the forest. Any creature that eats one will turn into a werewolf."

Drake frowned. "Is there a way to undo a werewolf curse?"

"I am not sure," Brighteye replied.

"Our parents teach us a rhyme about werewolves that could be helpful," Oskar added. "'The werewolf will bring only danger and doom, unless it is stopped by the dragon's bloom.'"

"Dragon's bloom . . ." Brighteye repeated.

"Nobody knows exactly what it means," Oskar said. "I think it has something to do with the Legendary Dragon of Stellburg."

Drake's head suddenly filled with Worm's words:

Wildroot is very excited. The Flower Dragons have a special power called Bloom. He thinks the rhyme means that Bloom can stop the werewolf! But they must perform Bloom in bright sunlight. What if the werewolf attacks at night?

Drake repeated Worm's words. Then he said, "The Flower Dragons' Bloom power might be the key to stopping the monster. But if the werewolf comes at night, we're doomed."

Ana smiled and looked at Kepri. "Let's show them what you can do!"

DANCING DRAGONS

Kepri nodded to Ana and soared up into the sky, over the Valley of Starflowers.

Wildroot and the tribe of Flower Dragons gazed up at the Sun Dragon. Then Kepri opened her mouth, and a wide beam of soft, warm sunlight streamed out.

The Flower Dragons closed their eyes and drank in the warmth. Then they opened their eyes and began to move. They formed a circle. Each dragon began to twirl and spin and leap.

"They're dancing!" Ana called out from above. She stared at them, spellbound.

"Flower Dragons eat sunlight. It powers them up," Drake remembered. "Kepri's light must be giving them extra energy."

"Incredible!" Brighteye said, fluttering her wings. "They will be able to perform Bloom even if the werewolf comes at night."

Oskar put his hands on his hips. "That's great. But a werewolf is a terrifying creature with sharp fangs and wicked claws. Even with some flowery blooming power, a bunch of tiny dancing dragons won't be able to fight a werewolf. We need to go back to the village, get pitchforks, and —"

"What about your rhyme?" Drake reminded him. "It says that the werewolf can be *stopped by the dragon's bloom*. That has to mean the Bloom power, doesn't it?"

Oskar frowned. "Maybe, but . . ."

Aaaaaaaeeeeeeeeeee!

A strange wail echoed through the valley.

Startled, Kepri quickly landed in the grass. The Flower Dragons stopped dancing.

Aaaaaaaeeeeeeeeeee!

"Is that the werewolf?" Ana asked.

A rustling sound came from the forest at the edge of the valley. Suddenly, an army of strange creatures emerged from the trees.

Aaaaaaaeeeeeeeeeee!

Oskar gasped. "The Finsterbuns!" he cried.

THE FINSTERBUNS!

The strange, small creatures charged forward. Drake squinted. They looked like rabbits, but different. Each one had leathery wings, sharp teeth, and antlers.

Drake gasped. "The Finsterbuns look like dangerous mini-monsters!"

"They're more weird than dangerous," Oskar explained. "They live in Finster Hollow, on the other side of the village. We stay away from them. If you touch one, you'll sprout furry bunny ears and a fluffy tail! Old Man John touched one when he was a boy, and he still wears a hat all the time."

Ana took a step back. "That is definitely weird!"

Aaaaaaaeeeeeeeeeeee!

Hundreds of Finsterbuns — more than Drake could count — raced onto the field and quickly began munching on starflowers.

"*Chee! Chee! Chee!*" Wildroot chirped in alarm and jumped on Worm's neck.

Seconds later, Drake heard Worm:

Wildroot says that if the Finsterbuns are not stopped, they will eat all the starflowers.

Drake remembered Wildroot saying that starflower nectar is what feeds the Flower Dragons' powers. Without the nectar, the dragons couldn't perform Bloom!

"We have to stop the Finsterbuns from eating the starflowers!" Drake cried. "Worm, freeze them!"

Worm's eyes began to glow bright green. All the Finsterbuns stopped moving.

Drake looked at Ana and Oskar. "Worm can't hold them like this for long. We need to find a way to get rid of them without hurting them."

"Why did they come here in the first place?" Ana wondered.

Just then, Brighteye flew over.

"I have had another vision," she said. "The werewolf entered Finster Hollow earlier today, and the Finsterbuns fled. It is very close now. It will be here by nightfall."

"Then we need to get these Finsterbuns out of here, fast!" Drake said. "The Flower Dragons need to feed on starflowers to get ready for the werewolf!"

Oskar's eyes lit up. "I know! The Finsterbuns are clearly hungry. We can lead them to the big field of chamomile flowers that's between here and the village. There is plenty of chamomile in the mountains, so the Finsterbuns can eat all they want."

"I think the Finsterbuns might follow the Flower Dragons if they start dancing again," Ana suggested. "I know I couldn't take my eyes off them."

Drake nodded. "It's worth a try."

Brighteye fluttered her wings. "I will ask the Flower Dragons to follow Kepri," she said, and then she flew off.

Ana jumped on Kepri's back. "Let's fly!"

Kepri flew to the group of frozen Finsterbuns. She streamed sunlight in front of them, and the Flower Dragons flocked to the light. Once again, they began to dance.

"All right, Worm. Unfreeze the Finsterbuns!" Drake yelled.

Worm's eyes stopped glowing. The weird creatures started moving again. They munched on the flowers.

Then they noticed the Flower Dragons, and their heads all turned at once.

"Kepri, forward!" Ana cried.

Kepri slowly flew toward the chamomile field. The Flower Dragon tribe danced after her. And one by one, the Finsterbuns hopped after them.

Drake grinned. "It's working! Kepri and the Flower Dragons are leading the Finsterbuns away from the Valley of Starflowers!"

NIGHT FALLS

Drake and Oskar walked behind the hopping Finsterbuns. Wildroot danced on Worm's neck as the Earth Dragon crawled along.

"Worm, thank you for freezing those Finsterbuns," Drake said.

Oskar sighed. "Your dragon has very amazing powers. You are lucky to be his Dragon Master."

"I am," Drake agreed. "But I had no idea how powerful he was when we first met. Worm surprised me."

"I do not think Wildroot will surprise me," Oskar said, looking at his dragon.

"Listen, the Dragon Stone chooses every Dragon Master for a reason," Drake said. "There's a reason why it chose you. You knew the poem about the dragon's bloom. It was your idea to bring the Finsterbuns to the chamomile field. And the danger isn't over yet — who knows what else you and Wildroot will do?"

Oskar frowned and didn't reply.

When they finally reached the chamomile field, Kepri stopped her sunlight. The Flower Dragons stopped dancing, and the Finsterbuns sniffed the air. Then they began munching on the chamomile flowers.

Ana swooped down on Kepri and landed beside Worm. "We did it!" she cried.

Drake gazed at the sky. "It's almost sunset. We should hurry back to the valley."

Ana grinned at the Flower Dragons. "Who wants a ride?" she asked. Several of the dragons happily climbed on Kepri's back. The Sun Dragon took off, flying low.

When everyone returned to the valley, Drake gathered the Flower Dragons together.

"Worm, please tell them to get ready for the werewolf. They should drink lots of starflower nectar to power up," Drake instructed.

Worm nodded.

Soon, the Flower Dragons spread out across the field and began to sip the nectar.

Oskar took off his backpack. "I brought some food for my trip to find my father. We should all eat something."

As the sun went down, Ana built a small fire in a clearing on the edge of the flowers. The three Dragon Masters sat near it, watching the flames as they ate. Worm, Kepri, and Wildroot stayed close by.

"This plan is madness," Oskar said. "There is a werewolf on the way! We need weapons."

"I think Wildroot and the rest of the Flower Dragons will come through," Drake told him.

"Yes," Ana agreed. "I have seen dragons do some really amazing things."

Oskar looked up at the stars. "I certainly hope their power works so we can go look for my father soon."

"Wildroot can come with us," Drake said. "I'm sure you two will bond on the trip."

Oskar shrugged. "Maybe. Wildroot is very cute, but I have always dreamed of being Dragon Master of a big, strong dragon, like the Legendary Dragon of Stellburg."

Drake saw Wildroot frown.

The little dragon hopped off Worm and walked away.

Drake sighed. "Oskar, I think —"

OWWWWWWWOOOOOOOOOOOOO!

A howl came from the forest. Drake felt a chill deep in his bones.

Oskar jumped up. "The werewolf is here!"

12

UNDER ATTACK!

Shaking in fear, the Flower Dragons rushed toward the Dragon Masters. Brighteye flew over to Drake.

"We must wait until the werewolf is in sight to perform Bloom," she told him. "Wildroot can command the Flower Dragons when it is time."

OWWWWWWWOOOOOOOOOOOOO!
The werewolf howled again.

Drake's head snapped to the right. "That howl came from another direction. Are there two werewolves?"

The creature is circling us, Worm told him. *It will force us into a small group so that it can attack us all at once.*

"Can you sense where it is and freeze it?" Drake asked.

It is moving too fast right now, Worm replied. *Perhaps when it gets closer.*

OWWWWWWWOOOOOOOOOOOOO!

The howl was louder this time. The hair stood up on Drake's arms.

"The werewolf is circling us!" Drake yelled. "Ana, get Kepri in place to charge up the Flower Dragons."

Ana jumped on Kepri's back. "Kepri, fly!"

Wildroot and the rest of the Flower Dragons grouped together. Worm, Drake, and Oskar stood near the tiny dragons, keeping an eye out for the werewolf.

OWWWWWWWOOOOOOOOOOOOO!

Drake, the werewolf will attack any minute, Worm warned.

But before Drake could warn the others, the werewolf charged at them, snarling and snapping its jaws. For a second, Drake couldn't breathe. The creature was as big as a horse, with muscles rippling under shaggy brown fur. Two red eyes glowed on its face, and rows of yellow, sharp teeth filled its huge mouth.

Drake shook off his fear. "Worm, freeze it!" he yelled.

Worm's eyes began to glow, but the werewolf was faster. It leapt through the air and tackled Worm, knocking him to the ground! It snarled and unfurled its jagged claws.

Overhead, Ana cried out, "Kepri, sunlight!"

A burst of bright golden light lit up the night, distracting the werewolf. Kepri flew in a tight circle around the Flower Dragons, focusing her light on them.

"Dragons, soak up the sunlight!" Brighteye called out.

The Flower Dragons lifted their faces to the sunlight...

GRRRRRRRRRRRRRRRRR!

The beast leapt away from Worm. It jumped over the Earth Dragon and lunged toward the terrified Flower Dragons.

"Worm! Worm! Are you all right?" Drake cried, running to his dragon.

Oskar dashed past Drake and jumped in between the werewolf and the Flower Dragons. "Leave these dragons alone, you monster!" he yelled.

BLOOM

The werewolf lunged at Oskar, snapping its jaws.

"Oskar!" Drake yelled.

The werewolf's body glowed green, and it stopped in midair. Drake gasped and looked at Worm. The dragon's eyes were open and shining with green light.

"Good work, Worm!" Drake cried.

Oskar's face was pale. He turned to Drake. "What now?"

Drake heard Worm's voice in his head:

This werewolf has powerful energy. I can't keep it frozen much longer. The Flower Dragons must perform Bloom.

"Ask Wildroot to give the Flower Dragons the command, Worm," Drake instructed.

Suddenly, Wildroot climbed onto Oskar's arm. Oskar's Dragon Stone began to glow. His mouth dropped open.

"I can hear Wildroot in my head!" he said, turning to his Flower Dragon. "The Flower Dragons are ready. But Worm must let go of the werewolf for their Bloom power to work."

Oskar looked into Wildroot's eyes. "I know you can do it! And I will be here to protect you if you need me."

Wildroot nodded.

Brighteye landed on Oskar's shoulder. "You and Wildroot are ready to lead the Flower Dragons."

Oskar smiled proudly. "Okay, Wildroot, tell the dragons to perform Bloom!"

The Flower Dragons began to glow with soft white light. The petals on top of each one's head opened up. A sweet scent traveled across the air.

"They're ready!" Oskar announced.

"Worm, unfreeze the werewolf now!" Drake yelled.

The green glow in Worm's eyes faded. The werewolf landed on the grass and snarled. Then it sniffed the air.

The creature collapsed to the ground.

"I think it's working!" Oskar cried, and Drake and Ana cheered. But then the werewolf slowly began to rise, growling...

Suddenly, Wildroot ran toward the werewolf.

"Wildroot, what are you doing?" Oskar yelled.

Wildroot jumped on the werewolf's back! The dragon's body started glowing brightly, and the wolf's nose twitched from the flowery smell.

White light spread across the werewolf. Then the creature became still.

In a flash, the light exploded! Drake had to shield his eyes from the brightness. When the light faded, he saw a man lying in the grass where the werewolf had been. A man with blond, wavy hair.

CHAPTER 14

THE TRAVELER'S TALE

Father!" Oskar cried.

Dazed, the man sat up. He stared at Oskar.

"Son!" he cried, and Oskar ran into his arms.

They both sobbed.

Ana and Kepri flew down from the sky. Wildroot and the Flower Dragons gathered around Oskar and his father.

Drake rushed over to them, shaking his head. "Oskar, is this really your father? But how —"

"I am not sure what happened to me," the man said, standing up.

"You have been missing for one month, since you left for Graystone Castle," Oskar explained.

His father nodded. "It's coming back to me. I was returning from the castle when I got lost in The Dark Forest. I became so hungry that I ate some strange white berries..."

"Moonberries are white!" Ana cried. "They're what turned you into a werewolf!"

Oskar's father shuddered. "To think I became that foul creature. But how ... how did you save me?"

"I am a Dragon Master now, Father," Oskar explained. "My dragon, Wildroot, and the rest of his tribe saved you. They used their powers to undo the terrible curse."

Oskar's father gazed at the Flower Dragons in wonder. "Thank you all," he said. He looked at his son. "I know it is late, but I would like to get back to Stellburg."

"Of course. The village is only about an hour's walk from here," Oskar said. "Wildroot, will you come with us?"

Wildroot climbed onto Oskar's arm, and the boy grinned.

"I can't wait to show you off to the villagers. Maybe they'll even build you a statue," he said. "Stellburg has a brave new dragon protector!"

Brighteye flew in front of Oskar. A magical ball of light glowed on the end of her wand. "I will come with you and light your way before I head back to the forest."

Oskar turned to his new friends. "Thank you, Drake and Ana," he said. "I hope one day I can be a great Dragon Master like you both are."

Ana grinned. "I'm sure you will."

Drake looked at his dragon. "Worm, time to go home!"

DIEGO'S IDEA

orm transported Drake, Ana, and Kepri
to Bracken.

When they appeared in the Training Room,
they heard laughter from down the hall.

Drake and Ana ran to the Dragon Masters' classroom. Griffith's wizard friend, Diego, was seated at the table with Griffith, Bo, and Rori.

Rori jumped up. "Drake! Ana! How did it go? Did you stop the red-eyed monster?"

"We did!" Ana replied. "And we also found Wildroot's Dragon Master, Oskar. He and Wildroot made a connection."

Griffith nodded. "Excellent. I know a wizard in the Lofty Mountains who can help Oskar and Wildroot learn to work together. I will contact her."

"Tell us about the monster!" Bo asked Drake.

"It's a long story," Drake said, taking a seat. He yawned. "And I'm pretty tired. It seems like Worm and I have been going nonstop ever since Astrid got loose."

Diego smiled. "That's exactly why I'm here, Drake! Carlos is very fond of you. He will never forget when you and Worm came to the Land of Aragon to tell him he was a Dragon Master. He would like you both to come for a visit."

Drake remembered that trip well. He thought of the smell of the salt air and the sandy beach where Diego and Carlos lived. It would be a very peaceful place to rest. And he liked Carlos and his dragon.

"How soon can we leave?" Drake asked, grinning. "I can't wait to see Carlos and Lalo the Lightning Dragon again!"

TRACEY WEST is a *New York Times* bestselling children's book author. Some of her ancestors came from a land similar to Stellburg, with many local legends about dragons.

Tracey is the step-mom to three grown-up kids. She shares her home with her husband, dogs, chickens, and a garden full of worms. They live in the misty mountains of New York State, where it is easy to imagine dragons roaming free in the green hills.

GRAHAM HOWELLS lives with his wife and two sons in west Wales, a place full of castles and legends of wizards and dragons.

There are many stories about the dragons of Wales. One story tells of a large, legless dragon—sort of like Worm! Graham's home is also near where Merlin the great wizard is said to lie asleep in a crystal cave.

Graham has illustrated several books. He has created artwork for film, television, and board games, too. Graham also writes stories for children. In 2009, he won the Tir Na n'Og award for *Merlin's Magical Creatures*.

'DRAGON MASTERS
BLOOM OF THE FLOWER DRAGON

Questions and Activities

Ana is excited for Wildroot to see Kepri's powers. Why? Reread page 18.

At first, Oskar is not happy to be paired with Wildroot. Why not?

Brighteye is a forest sprite. Drake met sprites on a previous adventure, too. What type of sprites were they? (Psst! Do you have book 14? If so, turn to page 50.)

Starflowers are important to Flower Dragons. In the real world, caterpillars that turn into monarch butterflies only eat milkweed plants. Sadly, these plants are disappearing. Research monarch butterflies to learn how you can help!

What powers do you think the Legendary Dragon of Stellburg had? Draw a picture to show how this dragon's powers work.